Banjora

THE BAT THAT COULDN'T FLY

by

Doug E. Rivers

Grosvenor House
Publishing Limited

This book is published by
Grosvenor House Publishing Ltd
Link House
140 The Broadway, Tolworth, Surrey, KT6 7HT.
www.grosvenorhousepublishing.co.uk

This book is a work of fiction. Any resemblance to
people or events, past or present, is purely coincidental.

A CIP record for this book
is available from the British Library

ISBN 978-1-78623-639-5

With love and thanks to

Joshua

and his magic book

Preface by the author

Children of all ages enjoy a good story; whether they read it themselves or have it narrated to them.

My Grandson was three when Banjora first emerged into this world. It could be said that the story and child grew together.

It deals with non-judgemental friendship and support; during a difficult time of Banjora's young life. He is encouraged to overcome his shortcomings and fly like the other bats in his Colony. He shows great determination and courage to achieve his goal, which briefly puts his life at risk. Eventually this leads to self-discovery, unexpected challenges, new friendships and some exciting adventures.

Part 1

The bat that couldn't fly

Banjora sighed and gripped the branch he was hanging from, upside down, more tightly than ever. He had spent a sleepy day just hanging around, which was for him a very agreeable situation.

However, it was dusk and all around, or more correctly above, he could hear the stretching and flapping of countless wings. The **Colony**[1] was stirring and he knew it would soon be time to go.

'Here we go again,' he thought; 'maybe this time.'

The Colony was on the move and Banjora half released his grasp on the branch, but then quickly clung-on again.

---

[1] Banjora lives in a **Colony** of Grey Headed Fruit Bats in a tropical forest of Eastern Australia. Fruit bats are nocturnal, flying and feeding mostly at night. They have good eyesight and feed on flowers, nectar and overripe fruit. They have distinctive orange-brown fur and long dog-like faces, which is why many people call them 'flying foxes.'

All around bats were taking to the air in a rush of wind and wings.

It seemed like total chaos to Banjora and he wondered, yet again, why collisions never occurred as countless bats moved in and out of trees, branches and other bats. They were off to feed and Banjora's tummy rumbled in anticipation.

'As soon as it is a bit less crowded, I'll go,' he decided.

Some minutes later, when nearly all the bats had flown away, he finally let go and flapping his wings frantically, dropped into the bushes below.

"Ouch and bother," he cried, more in disappointment than pain. After all he had chosen to roost in the lower branches, not the high ones used by the other bats, so he did not fall too far. He was also surprisingly well-padded for a bat, which helped in falling situations.

"Hard luck Banjora, keep trying. You will get there in the end."

An encouraging voice came from above and he saw Yindi, a young female bat, waving as she flew over.

He got up, brushed himself down and set off. It might take him half an hour to catch up, but there was always plenty of food and other bats, like Yindi, would look out for him and save him some fruit or flowers.

He quite liked being on the ground, particularly as it helped get the blood back into his legs, which were now beneath him. They tingled for a while, but he was soon hopping along, surprisingly quite quickly and he hummed a little tune as he went. He could not remember where he had heard this tune, but he always felt warm and safe when he hummed it.

Soon he reached the edge of the plantation of fruit trees that was tonight's dining place for the Colony. He started to climb an appetising looking tree.

"Not that one silly, that's a gum tree. The fruit is up here."

It was Yindi's voice again and she was calling from high in a nearby fruit tree.

He crossed the clearing and climbed up. Soon he was hanging upside down beside her and he said, "Thanks, I don't know why I did that."

"You were not concentrating; that's your problem. You need to concentrate to find food… and to fly," she added hopefully; but he was not listening as he tucked into the fruit that was all around him in the branches. He was a messy eater and his face and body were heavily stained by the fruit juices, from reddish brown to almost black in places.

On the way back he thought about his earlier fall. It had hurt a bit more than usual. He would have to check that the pile of leaf litter he had placed under his special bush to cushion his landing, had not become flattened.

To his surprise, it wasn't there anymore. He rooted around in the nearby bushes and found some more, which he carefully placed under the bush directly beneath his sleeping branch. Then he climbed up into the roosting tree, clambered along the lower branch and, checking his position in relation to the bush and pile of leaf litter below, swung upside down and went to sleep, almost at once. He was exhausted.

Some weeks went by, but Banjora's attempts to fly always ended in failure. He tried everything he could, watching the other bats and copying their actions. When it was hot they would open their wings and flap them like fans to cool down. When it was cold they wrapped their wings tightly around their bodies, like a blanket. Just before they took flight each evening they stretched and flapped their wings and then flew effortlessly away.

Banjora's somewhat stunted wings made poor fans and it was just as well that he didn't feel the cold because they were useless as a blanket, being neither long enough nor wide enough to wrap around anything much at all. Sadly, his attempts at flapping and stretching vigorously, just before take-off, still resulted in the short fall into the bush below; and somebody or something kept taking his leaf litter.

"I don't understand what's going on," he told Yindi.

"Well," she said hopefully, "any day now you will fly and you won't need it anymore."

The bats were now feeding on forest trees, as the local plantation farmer had taken exception to his fruit being eaten and things could get nasty.

The leader of the Colony had overheard him talking to one of his men.

"We will have to get some netting up to stop them flying foxes; and if I see that 'kwala' in my trees again, I'll shoot him for sure."

The Colony leader was wise and knew when to move on. They could always go back once any nets had been removed. As a result, Banjora's walks to feed were getting longer and more tiring.

"I think I will try some local food," he said to Yindi one evening.

Yindi would have none of it. She had her heart set on becoming Banjora's partner and was not going to allow him to fade away.

"You'll die if you don't eat properly," she grumbled and refused to fly off to feed until she had seen him fly to the ground and set off.

Now this was becoming very, very embarrassing for Banjora.

'But it's only because she cares for me,' he thought, cheering up a little.

Next morning Yindi flew down to his branch and hung upside down beside him. She noticed how big he was getting and was concerned. Even though he was always last to set off, once he reached the feeding trees he was a bit of a glutton, eating far more than the other bats.

"Perhaps you should lose some weight," she said.

"Perhaps weight is the problem with your flying."

"Not to mention these useless wings," he grumbled back at her, waving them up and down.

They were both silent for a while and Yindi was thinking that Banjora was not as bat-looking as might be expected of a maturing young fruit bat. Somewhat fatter and furrier and ….

she fell asleep thinking about this.

That evening she did not wait for Banjora to set off as he had promised faithfully to follow along to the feeding trees. She was sure he would not break his promise.

Despite the promise to Yindi, Banjora still dithered and delayed. He was getting really fed up with this falling business. Eventually he just took the plunge.

"Yikes that hurt," a high pitched if slightly muffled voice came from under Banjora.

Banjora rolled sideways off something lumpy in his leaf litter. He saw a strange looking little creature straightening out its' ears and long tail.

"Sorry," he said.

"Not me night, not me night at all," squeaked the stranger.

"First, I have to cope with somebody stealing me nest, not just once, but time and time again and now this. Or, to be more precise, ya."

He glared at Banjora.

"Sorry," said Banjora again, somewhat nervously. Then with more confidence he added, "You're not the only one losing things. My landing pad keeps going missing."

The two gave each other the once-over. The smaller of the two had long back legs, a long tail, a pointy snout and greyish, but not abundant fur. For those familiar with kangaroos, he was a bit like one of those, but much, much, much smaller.

The larger was plumpish and almost cuddly. He had thick reddish grey fur. His ears were a little floppy and his dark eyes were set above a long nose.

Deciding that the larger creature in front of him was probably not dangerous; unless of course it fell on you, the little one introduced himself.

"G'day. I'm Rufus, pleased to meet ya."

"Same here, I'm Banjora," then apologetically, "I'm sorry I flew down on you."

Rufus looked a bit puzzled by this remark.

"What are you?" asked Banjora, but without waiting for a reply started to say, "I'm a fruit ba...."

"I know what ya are," interrupted Rufus, rather rudely.

"I recognise ya now, but why don't ya know me. We sorts have lived around each other for years and years and years. I'm a Kangaroo Rat; and I've lost me bed. Any ideas how it came to be under this bush?" he added, with more than a hint of suspicion in his eyes.

"Of course," said Banjora "I put it there."

"That's unbelievable," retorted an astounded Rufus.

"Ya don't sleep in a ground nest, so why do ya keep taking me bed and putting it under this bush?"

"It is not a bed it's a landing pad. I didn't know you were using it as a nest and in any case, I had it first and I need it to land on until I can fly properly ...." Banjora tailed off.

"Of all the crazy excuses for nest-napping, that's the most stupendously, incredibly improbable one I have ever heard!" shrieked Rufus. Then he added angrily, "And ya'll never fly; no way, not a chance!"

He hopped off into the underbrush, full of indignation.

'Oh dear, that didn't go too well,' thought Banjora.

This unfortunate encounter had, most surprisingly, caused Banjora to lose his appetite, so he climbed back into his tree to think, rest and sleep. Not for the first time he dreamed a strange dream about flying eucalyptus leaves that tweeted like birds and nested in gum trees.

In the morning he was woken by Yindi whispering in his ear.

"We've got to talk," she murmured. "You know, about our future. How can we be together if you can't fly? You know how much I care about you. You just have to fly; for both of us."

Banjora was now fully awake and very determined to fly for Yindi. He also wanted to show that Rufus character that he, Banjora, could and would do it.

"Right, just watch me fly," he said; suddenly full of confidence and grit.

"But first to the very top of this tree; to the topmost branch. This will give me room to get properly airborne. That's been the problem before; not enough airspace."

"My hero," sighed Yindi, looking on in admiration.

Banjora started to climb, slowly but steadily. Now this was a very tall tree, almost thirty metres high. Any creature jumping from the top and failing to fly would be very badly injured, or more likely killed by the fall.

Yindi watched in hope and expectation.

"Fly for me," she called out after him.

"He has about as much chance of flying as *Ayers Rock*.[2]"

---

[2] *Ayres Rock* – Located in Central Australia the rock is over 300 metres high and 8 kilometres around. It is a sacred place for the Aboriginal Tribes, who call it 'ULURU'

A squeaky yell came from Rufus who had been watching below.

"He'll kill himself from up there. What does he think he is; a bird, a plane, a balloon."

Yindi looked down and saw the strange little creature that Banjora had fallen upon the previous evening.

"He knows he is a fruit bat and therefore he will fly," she said almost confidently.

"Fruit bat, more like fruitcake. He is a koala and they don't fly. I tell ya he will die!"

Yindi, now confused, concerned and worried looked up to see Banjora balancing on the top branch. He no longer seemed so confident and he wobbled as he hesitated.

"Wait," she shrieked, "please don't jump!"

Alas, too late. Banjora jumped out of the tree, flapping wildly. Yindi could not look and closed her eyes tight shut. She sobbed, wrapping her head under her wings and was inconsolable, convinced that Banjora would die and that it was all her fault.

As he climbed the tree, a very determined Banjora passed, but did not notice, a high-level meeting of three Elders of the Colony which had been called by Matong, their leader. They were discussing the urgent need to tell both Banjora and young Yindi the truth and did not see Banjora climb by on the other side of the tree.

Suddenly, they were alerted by Yindi's shrieks. Looking up they saw Banjora about to jump from the tree top. They flapped into action like a well drilled aerobatics team.

At that same moment Banjora leapt into space.

Eyes shut, arms flapping vigorously, he felt air rushing by his face.

'Am I flying,' he wondered, when suddenly the rush of air slowed significantly.

He opened his eyes and saw, to his astonishment, that he was no longer falling, but now lifting slowly into the sky. Then he realised that he had stopped flapping. He quickly started again.

"There's no need for that, Banjora; we've got you now."

He twisted his head and saw that Matong and two Elders each had a hold of the fur on his back and were flapping their wings as one, to keep him up. He was so upset.

"Why can't I fly; what's wrong with me?"

"There's nothing wrong with you, Banjora. So just enjoy the ride and we will take you to a suitable tree where we can explain everything," replied Matong.

'"Yes please and soon," said the other two bats. "He's got so heavy."

The bats flew over to a big eucalyptus, also known as a gum tree. Here they carefully put Banjora into the treetop. Banjora waited for them to land.

When all three bats were hanging on a branch just above him Banjora started to climb up, but was told to stay as he was, sitting on a branch. Oddly, he felt very comfortable like this.

Matong then explained to Banjora how the bats had found him, still a very small baby, abandoned in a tree nest.

They suspected that his parents had been killed or taken by poachers (very bad humans) to sell them as pets. At that time, they had been the only family of koalas left in that area, so the bats had fed him and kept him safe. As he became bigger and stronger, they had been amused at his attempts to behave like a bat.

"We should have told you this much sooner, but you seemed so happy we didn't have the heart to tell you the truth," said Matong.

"So, if I am not a bat, what am I," asked Banjora, "and why didn't Yindi know this?"

Matong reassured him. "You are a young koala bear and as Yindi has never seen one before, she just came to think of you as another special kind of fruit bat."

"Be reassured that you are a very fine koala bear," said the other two, "and, of course, still one of our family, so please never forget this."

They then flew off, leaving Matong to answer Banjora's many questions about koalas, bats, jumping rats, eucalyptus dreams and, well, almost everything.

"This flying lark is fun, but a bit scary."

Yindi jumped at the sound of Banjora's voice.

"It cannot be you, you're dead; are you a ghost?" she stuttered.

"No Yindi, it is me and I'm OK. I'm really fine and look; still all in one piece."

She reluctantly squeezed open her eyes and saw it was so. She also noticed that he was not hanging upside down, but squatting on a branch on his back legs. She had never seen him looking quite so relaxed.

"And I've got lots to tell you. I hope you won't be too disappointed...."

"Mate that was amazing, stupendous," a squeaky voice interrupted from below. Yindi and Banjora looked down to see Rufus struggling up the tree.

"Remind me, what's ya name again, so I can tell all me chums about ya; the first flying koala bear, or is it ba aa aa at...."

As he started to fall Banjora grabbed his long tail and pulled him back up to the branch.

"Thanks mate, I owe ya. Could'a been a gonner, right then an' there."

Straightening his ruffled fur, Rufus got comfortable on the branch.

"Anyway, what's ya name and whose ya friend?"

"I am Banjora and this is Yindi. Yindi this is Rufus; he's a kind of jumping rat."

"Hello Rufus," she responded, "but did you just say that Banjora flew?"

"I surely did. Saw it me self. One second he was dropping like a stone. I couldn't look. Closed me eyes but had to look again. When I opened 'em, he had spread great black wings and was flying as high as the moon. Flew off over those big trees he did," pointing. "It was truly awesome."

Rufus gave a big sigh at the memory of it.

"Is it true, can you really fly, Banjora?" asked Yindi with excitement in her voice.

"I just told ya he can, saw it meself and….mmm." Banjora put a paw over Rufus' mouth.

"If you will just stop talking for one minute I will explain everything. Promise to keep quiet."

This was an instruction from Banjora, not a request.

"I'll be quiet as a mouse, oops rat… " Rufus fell silent as Banjora raised his paw.

Now Yindi interrupted, "But how did you do it; how did you fly, Banjora?"

"I am so sorry Yindi, but I didn't and I can't. Matong and two Elders flew out and grabbed me; otherwise I would probably have died from the fall. It was their wings that Rufus saw.

Matong explained everything to me in the big eucalyptus tree; by the way, I just love the taste of the eucalyptus leaves and…"

"Aaargh," said Rufus, "they're inedible and…mmm."

Banjoras' paw covered his mouth once more.

It took Banjora much of the night, with frequent interruptions from Rufus, to tell the full story; before declaring:

"I am Banjora a koala bear. Koalas live in eucalyptus trees, eat eucalyptus leaves, sleep a lot and do not fly at all.

We don't hang upside down to sleep and don't walk on the ground; well not that much, anyway."

"That's just what I tried to tell ya when we first met," said Rufus.

"I was so worried Banjora, but it all begins to make sense, I think," said Yindi, still trying to come to terms with Banjora's story.

"Yes, I suppose so; but this has been hard for me to take in. I so wanted to be a good bat and fly with you, Yindi."

Banjora tried to hide the sadness in his voice as he realised that not only could he not fly but he could not be Yindi's partner.

Then he brightened up as he remembered the good things he had learned.

He knew who he was, what he was, why he was different and, importantly, why he could not fly. In time he hoped to meet other koalas and maybe find his real Mum and Dad. Meanwhile he had the Colony of bats as his special family and he truly hoped that he and Yindi would always remain friends.

Best of all he was alive; not a crumpled heap on the ground.

He also thought he may have found a new and interesting friend in Rufus.

Yes, all was well.

Banjora hung upside down next to a sleepy, still slightly bemused young female bat.

"In time all will be fine, Yindi and I promise we will always be the best of friends."

Rufus hung there too; by his tail.

"Oh good, it's morning," he said.

"Time to sleep."

Part 2

The rescue

Banjora sighed a deep and very satisfying sigh as he adjusted his position on the branch of the eucalyptus tree, where he now rested in complete koala-comfort.

He had quickly adjusted to life as a koala bear; not a bat.

He no longer slept hanging upside down from a branch. He didn't eat much fruit anymore, as a result of which his chest fur and arms had slowly lost the black-red stains produced by the fruits' juices. These stains had once made him look a bit bat-like, but his fur was now a greyish brown colour all over, except for the creamy white flash on his chest.

Yes, now very koala-looking.

He had lost weight too. The eucalyptus leaves that he now so loved to eat had made him stronger and fitter and slimmer, but like all koalas he still slept a lot, particularly during the day.

His legs no longer tingled and ached as before. This was the result of not hanging upside down to sleep and of course, as he knew he was not a fruit bat, flying was unnecessary.

Well, perhaps not necessary, but Banjora had, on reflection, enjoyed his one 'flying' experience and wished he could do it again. This 'flying' experience, as you may recall, had occurred when Banjora, still believing he was a bat, had made a desperate attempt to fly by leaping from the top of the very tall bat roosting tree.

The sigh he now made was one of regret. He so missed his parents, even though he could barely remember them.

But flying had been fun. He sighed again.

"What's up mate?" said a squeaky voice from nearby.

Banjora turned to see Rufus, the kangaroo rat, emerging from his sleeping hole. He was rubbing his eyes with his short front paws. "Why the big sighs?"

As a result of his previous adventures, Banjora had met and become friends with Rufus. Rufus had decided to spend more time with Banjora so he had moved from his ground burrow to a new nest, which he made up in a hollow in the eucalyptus tree where Banjora now spent most of his time. Rufus was still not completely convinced that Banjora could not fly and felt that by staying close to him he would be rewarded with another wonderful flying display. The two talked about it quite often; Banjora always trying to explain why he could not fly; whilst Rufus argued that great benefits would come to a koala bear that could actually fly.

"Ya could join a circus and see the world. Be a big celebrity. I could be ya manager. I know ya miss it, don't ya."

Banjora could not deny that flying had been a great experience, particularly as the alternative had been crashing into the ground at great speed and probably dying. Yes, he did miss it, but knew it was impossible for a koala to fly.

Yindi, the young female fruit bat, visited Banjora each evening and some mornings too.

She also had once believed he was a young, if slightly different, fruit bat and had regularly encouraged him to keep trying to fly.

Both had now overcome their disappointment that they could not be partners and were, instead, great friends. They spent a lot of time talking about their memories of Banjora trying to fly and how funny it all now seemed.

"But I think you do miss it, don't you?" Yindi said on more than one occasion.

"Yes, I do, but even though I have lost a lot of weight, these little arms and this body are not meant to fly," was always Banjoras' response.

While Banjora slept mostly during the day, he always made sure he was awake for his morning and evening meetings with Yindi and Rufus.

Each evening Rufus had to go down to the forest floor to eat and catch up with his friends and family in the ground burrows, but he always found time to talk with

Banjora before he left and again when he returned each morning. Yindi dropped in on her way to feed at night and quite often on her return.

Banjora also fed at night, so once Yindi and Rufus had departed he would make his way up into the branches above and feast slowly, so slowly, on his favourite eucalyptus leaves.

One evening Yindi brought a young male fruit bat along with her. She introduced him as Jungai. He was a very lively and happy young bat. Banjora liked him immediately.

"I hear you once flew," said Jungai.

"That's right mate, saw it meself," this came from Rufus who had just emerged from his nest hollow.

Banjora explained how he had only flown with the aid of the three Elders. Jungai understood this at once, but as he loved flying so much himself, he thought that Banjora must want to fly again. He said, "Wouldn't you like to have another go?"

Banjora just shrugged in reply; it was after all impossible.

A little while later the two bats flew off to feed, but not before Jungai had promised to think about how Banjora might fly again. A grumpy Rufus, just a bit jealous of this newcomer, was for once very sceptical about Banjora being able to fly again.

"He's all wings and waffle. I tell ya he'll never get ya airborne."

Later, Banjora recalled Rufus' change of tune, but let any thoughts of it pass as he drifted off into sleep.

Not for the first time he dreamed of flying to faraway places where other koalas lived endlessly happy lives.

Jungai was as good as his word. After feeding each night, he began searching around the forest edges for suitable items for his plan. He found a ball of old twine, dropped by a careless farm worker and some light but very strong branches. He took these to a safe place and when he had gathered enough, he asked a friend Twister, the Bower bird, who was very good at making things, if he could put these together to form a sort of cradle.

The Bower bird is an interesting chap. The male bird constructs tall, almost tunnel shaped arches made out of sticks and twigs, which he decorates with objects such as berries, cones and bits of colourful plastic. His plan is to attract a female mate.

Now this takes a lot of time and effort and Twisters' efforts of late had not been fruitful. He had not attracted a female; so he did not hesitate and agreed to build the cradle. He thought he would enjoy a new challenge and it would take his mind off recent failures in the Bower-building business.

When the cradle was finished, Jungai tried to persuade two young male bats to volunteer as cradle-flyers.

These two thought the idea was completely mad, but they were young and adventurous, so they eventually agreed.

Jungai taught them how to support the cradle by holding the twine which was attached to it. At first, they were a bit clumsy, almost bumping into each other as they flew side by side, but they soon mastered the technique and became a very competent team.

"I shall call this the 3bp flying-cradle," said Jungai, after their fifth successful test flight.

"What's 3bp?" asked the other two.

"Three bat powered," replied Jungai, then after a pause asked,

"are you ready for the real thing?"

"More than ready, let's do it."

Jungai felt a sense of elation.

"Now for some passengers!" he yelled.

"Time to go flying," Jungai called out to a sleepy Banjora early one bright morning.

The Sun had just started to peep over the distant horizon.

Banjora looked on in disbelief and some fear.

"I'm not getting in that," he said.

"C'mon mate, it will be great!" shouted Rufus, who emerged from his hollow. He jumped straight in.

Banjora saw that it seemed to work, so when the bats flew up once more, he also jumped in.

"Woaa," said the three bats as the extra weight made them drop down; but they soon recovered by coordinating their flying and set off, soaring over the tallest of the nearby trees.

"What a buzz, brilliant, stupendous," whooped a delighted Rufus.

Banjora quietly agreed as his initial fears were forgotten. This was fun indeed.

After this first successful flight, weekly trips followed.

Jungai noticed that these flights were quite tiring and decided that whilst the '3bp' was alright for short trips, they would need more bats as cradle-flyers if they wanted to travel any long distances.

He discussed this with Twister the Bower bird, whom he found in very good spirits.

Twister had modified his latest bower-arch to include some of the features from the flying cradle, including bits of twine and he now had a mate. He was more than happy to take on this new challenge and very confident that he could make a cradle which more bats could fly. He immediately set about the task, using the spare twine and sticks left over from the first cradle. He also asked Jungai to find two extra-long sticks that he felt he would need to complete the job.

"I will make it so at least seven bats can fly it," said Twister.

Jungai smiled at the thought.

'Yes, a 7bp.'

Then one very early morning, before it was really light, a member of the original cradle-flyers-team disturbed Banjora, who had just finished feeding. The bat was shouting, flapping his wings wildly and was very, very agitated.

"You must come quickly. Yindi and Jungai and lots of others are trapped at the fruit farm. You must help; we can't get them free."

Now if we go back a couple of days to the fruit farm, we would have seen the farmer getting his men to lay rocket-propelled nets around the trees that the bats had recently started to feed in.

"I'll have the varmints now," said the farmer, who was named Moody. His name very much matched his personality. There was a gleam in his eyes. "Whoosh, rockets away, gotcha."

The following night as the bats fed in the same trees, Farmer Moody, hidden in an old bird-watchers tent, trembled in anticipation as he carefully lit the fuses to the rockets. They all had to go off together to fly the nets successfully and they did.

His crafty plan had worked and over fifty bats were now trapped in the nets.

"Get to it lads!" he yelled, as he struggled from the tent.

Five of his workers came out from hiding in nearby bushes and started to collect the unfortunate bats. They took them from the nets and placed them into sacks which were then roughly dumped onto the farm trailer.

The captive bats would certainly have come to a sudden and very unpleasant end, but for Daisy. She was Farmer Moody's only daughter and when she learned that he proposed to kill the bats, she screamed and screamed and screamed and SCREAMED until he promised, "Cross your heart and hope to die," not to do so.

As a result, the bats were released from the sacks inside an old barn, where the only door and window openings had been netted over, to prevent escape.

Farmer Moody had consoled his daughter, but what might he do next? No way would he let the bats go free. A plan was forming in his head; 'what if I make it look like I let 'em go, but actually dispose of 'em.'

He chuckled, as images of the farm incinerator kept creeping into his head. The outlook for the bats looked very bad, very bad indeed.

Banjora learned more about the capture as, with Rufus clinging to his back, he travelled overland to the farm. The young bat circled overhead. He was calmer now and explained that the bats were trapped in a barn.

Soon they could see the barn ahead and Banjora knew that they had to avoid the farm dog and get to the barn unnoticed, if they were to have any chance of getting the bats out. He also saw that Farmer Moody had posted one of his men with a gun, nearby, so any bat approaching the barn would be in danger of being shot. It was a tricky situation. Banjora sent the young bat off to feed and told him to keep away, for his own safety.

Then Banjora and Rufus, very carefully, started to creep round the edge of the field in which the old barn stood. They needed to approach it from the opposite side to where the farm worker sat with gun at the ready, so they would be out of sight.

Once, they had to stop dead, standing like statues as the farm dog, Big Rusty, came into the field to do his business. Sniffing the air Big Rusty peered towards them, but fortunately his eyesight was not so good anymore.

He was an old dog and he became distracted by thoughts of a large marrow-bone waiting in his kennel. He finished what he came for and went back to the comfort of his kennel and his bone.

"Phew that was close," whispered Rufus.

On reaching the barn Banjora and Rufus climbed carefully up towards a window opening. They found strong netting nailed across it. Banjora pulled at it but it hurt his paws.

Rufus started nibbling at the net, but after a few minutes he had barely made an impression.

"We need reinforcements. Hang on here, I'll be back."

Whilst he was away Banjora called quietly to Yindi, trapped inside the barn. She was astonished to see him. She begged him to be careful and not to get caught.

He explained the plan.

"Get everyone ready to go when we get this netting off. But in the meantime, keep them all as quiet as possible."

He climbed down to look for anything that would help cut the netting. He eventually found a piece of rough metal and climbed back up. To his amazement the netting was now covered in rats and mice of all shapes and sizes; each nibbling hard at a different piece. Rufus was in charge, encouraging and guiding them.

Three hours later many strands of the net had been chewed through.

'Just a few more and the bats can fly free,' thought Banjora.

Then, potential disaster loomed. He saw the man with the gun advancing towards the barn.

'He will see us for sure and all will be lost.'

Banjora told Rufus to get the netting open double-quick, while pointing to the oncoming man.

"I'll distract him."

Now koalas can move fast for short distances and this is just what Banjora did now. He dropped to the ground and set off hopping straight at and past the surprised worker, who turned and gave chase; and what a chase. Banjora had never moved so fast before and he managed to stay ahead of his pursuer. He had to climb a few fences and was almost caught, but evaded capture by scuttling through a large drainage pipe lying in the farmyard.

Things got worse when Big Rusty joined the chase and Banjora only avoided his snapping teeth by diving into a nearby hen-house.

The hens did not seem concerned by this ball of fur lying panting in their straw and one even tried to lay an egg on him.

Then Redrock the Rooster appeared. He was the lord of the hen-house and no furry stranger was going to invade his domain.

A raucous "cock-a-doodle-doo" was followed by several stinging pecks forcing Banjora to flee once more, but this time straight into the arms of the waiting farm worker.

"What's going on Sid?" asked Farmer Moody, who had just arrived.

"I caught this kwala by the barn. Had a heck of a job catching 'im."

"What about the bats, Sid, are they still secured? I've decided to dispose of them."

They were now approaching the barn. Banjora held his breath. Farmer Moody turned on his torch and peered in.

"What the…. gone, they have all gone!"

He rushed round to the window opening and saw the netting flapping loose. He saw it had been chewed through and grabbing Banjora he forced his mouth open.

"No, couldn't have been him."

"What shall we do with 'im Boss?"

"Shoot him. I bet he's the one that I've seen before in my fruit trees."

"Shoot what Daddy?"

Woken up by the noise of the chase, Daisy had come to see if the bats were safe.

Then she saw the empty barn and the captive Banjora and cried out, "Oooh lovely, wonderful Daddy, you've let them all go…. and is this bear for me?"

She reached out towards Banjora. What could her Father say.

So that was how Banjora became a pet for Daisy, albeit within an enclosure. But it had a small eucalyptus tree, water and some cuddly toys for company. Daisy was a thoughtful child.

Back at the bat Colony there were great celebrations for the escape. Much praise and thanks were given to Rufus and his friends who had successfully chewed through the netting.

But most of all the bats wanted to thank Banjora, for Rufus had explained how he had lured the man with the gun away from the barn, just in time.

So where was he now? He had not been seen for the last three days. Jungai volunteered to fly back to the farm to see if Banjora was safe. About an hour later he returned with the bad news that Banjora was in an enclosure and it had an electric fence on top, to stop him climbing out.

On the positive side, the girl-child at the farm was looking after him, so he did not seem to be in any immediate danger.

"He rescued us, so we must rescue him!" cried out Yindi.

"Yes, let's go now!" they all shouted.

"STOP!" Matong, the Colony Leader flew above them.

His voice rose above their shouting. Silence was immediate. All looked on and waited.

"We must have a plan if we are not going to end up in those nets again."

"Jungai and the Elders come with me now to discuss what we do next."

"The rest of you, get some sleep."

At the meeting the Elders could not agree on a suitable plan. It would put the Colony at risk if they continued to upset the farmer. Matong was quiet for some time and then spoke.

"I believe we must move the Colony to a new area and, sad as I am to say it, Banjora will have to remain with the girl-child."

"I have a suggestion.... how we can rescue Banjora, that is," Jungai said, hesitantly.

"We can get him out in the flying-cradle."

He described their recently successful flights.

"But that contraption is only good for short trips, you've said so yourself," argued one of the Elders, who had witnessed some of the flights.

"Not if we use the new seven bat cradle," replied Jungai; growing in confidence and now sure that his plan was good and would work.

He told them that Twister the Bower bird had recently completed the new cradle. It was ready to go.

"So, with a little training, seven of us can get him out, easy-peasy."

Jungai also suggested that he should fly in alone the night beforehand and let Banjora know what was happening. He would then be ready to jump into the cradle as soon as they arrived the following night.

Matong had serious doubts about this plan. He was now sure that the Colony must move far away from the farm, because the farmer would certainly give chase if Banjora escaped.

Matong was again quiet for some time.

The others respectfully stayed quiet.

Eventually Matong had made his decision.

"If we attempt this rescue and are successful, we will need to take Banjora far away to a place where the farmer cannot reach him. Somewhere he can be reunited with others of his kind. We owe him this. Now leave, we must sleep and then prepare our plans tomorrow."

He gave a final order.

"Tell all in the Colony of this decision and ensure no one goes anywhere near that farm without my authorisation."

Will they rescue Banjora?

Part 3

The journey

Banjora was a hero. He had carried out an amazing rescue with the help of his friend Rufus and loads of Rufus' friends and relations.

Over fifty fruit bats had been released from captivity and certain death at the hands of Farmer Moody.

But Banjora had been captured during the rescue and was now trapped in a compound.

Matong, the leader of the bat Colony and the Elders were meeting to decide what to do next. Jungai, a young male bat was with them. He had proposed they use a flying cradle to enable Banjora to escape from his enclosure.

"I believe the farmer will come looking for our roost and try to kill or capture all of us," said Matong.

"This is my plan. You Elders will take the Colony to the East, over the mountains into the forests on the other side, out of reach of that evil farmer. I will remain here with Jungai and six other young, strong males. Jungai will train them to fly the new cradle. Once I am happy that they are competent to fly it safely we can make an escape plan for Banjora."

"Will we fly him over the mountains too?" asked Jungai.

"No, we must fly him somewhere he will be safe. Somewhere where others of his kind can help and support him. I think that place lies to the West where humans have a large colony. At least I hope that is the way."

"Too right mate." Rufus climbed into view. He puffed from his exertions for it had been a long climb up the tree to where the bats were assembled.

"I've got a third cousin, twice removed. He's a wallaby; Waroo's his name. He was born in a zoo; that's where the humans keep animals. He got away and travelled into the scrub, then North round Big-water Lake. He lives on the forest edge to the West of here. The stories he can tell…"

"What is your point," said Matong, angry at being interrupted. Then he mellowed a little, as he recognised the newcomer.

"What help can you give us please, Rufus?"

"Well, Waroo told me that some koalas lived at the zoo, so if ya can get Banjora there, he'll be okaydokay. But it is a long journey across the scrubland and round the lake, particularly at this time of year, when the West wind can blow hard."

"What if we fly straight across the lake?" asked Jungai.

"Could save ya a hundred and fifty kilometres or more, but are ya sure it's on. That lake must be fifteen kilometres across right now."

"Well, Jungai, what do you think?" asked Matong.

"The farthest we have flown is about six kilometres, but that was only with three bats. I am sure that with seven bats as cradle-flyers we can more than double that distance."

Thus the escape plan was agreed.

Shortly after, the Elders lead the Colony away to the East, across the mountains to a new roost and feeding site.

Yindi, a close friend of Banjora, kept out of sight and stayed behind. She needed to know that he had escaped and also she wanted to say goodbye, personally.

Jungai and his six chosen cradle-flyers immediately started practice fights, with Rufus and a rock to represent Banjora, as passengers.

Jungai reported to Matong that the test flights had gone well.

Matong was pleased and said, "I shall personally fly to the farm tonight to let Banjora know what is to happen. This will ensure he will be ready and waiting in the top of his tree when you come for him tomorrow night."

Jungai had wanted to do this himself, but he knew better than to argue with Matong, for whom he had great love and respect.

Sensing the young bat's dilemma Matong explained.

"You are Captain of the flying team. It is important that you are unharmed and ready to lead the rescue. If I do not return, take care tomorrow night and approach with caution. Make sure Banjora is in position before you leave the cover of the trees."

Yindi, who had been hiding close by, spoke up, a little nervously.

"Matong, may I fly with you to the edge of the trees. I can watch as you go in and report back to Jungai."

Matong was surprised that Yindi was still around, but nodded in agreement. "But you must stay out of sight. Jungai must know what to expect when he arrives."

The nine bats flew off to feed after which Matong and Yindi flew on towards the farm. Jungai and the others flew back to the old roost to sleep. They found Rufus curled up in the flying-cradle and woke him.

'Ya didn't think I wasn't coming on the rescue too,' he said, then went straight back to sleep.

Meanwhile, Matong and Yindi approached the edge of the trees near to the farm. They could see the enclosure, but not Banjora. Where was he?

Yindi saw him first. He was in a bunch of leaves on a lower branch of his eucalyptus tree; feeding. Matong flew in, as quietly as possible and grabbed the branches. They were not very strong and almost broke under his weight. He was now hanging in full view, just below Banjora.

"Matong, what are you doing here?" whispered Banjora; for even in his state of shock that the Leader of the Colony was in his enclosure, he knew he must not wake Big Rusty, the farm dog.

Matong explained the plan and told Banjora he must be at the top of his tree the next night, ready for Jungai and his rescue team. Banjora nodded that he understood.

Then with a sharp crack, the branches supporting Matong gave way and plummeted downwards.

Big Rusty emerged from his kennel barking furiously.

Farmer Moody came rushing from the farmhouse wearing only his red one-piece long-johns and yellow woolly nightcap with a purple tassel. He was also carrying his shotgun.

Banjora could not resist a chuckle; the farmer looked so funny, but the chuckle ended abruptly.

Farmer Moody saw something flying above the enclosure and fired, twice.

"Bang! Bang!"

A very upset Yindi flew back into the old roost and found Jungai.

"I think the farmer shot Banjora and I don't know where Matong is. He might be dead too...." she sobbed.

"Yindi, please try to stop crying and tell me; did Matong get to speak with Banjora?"

Eventually, Yindi stopped sobbing long enough to say, "Yes, I think so."

"Then tonight is on, please get some rest and don't worry. I am sure Banjora and Matong are safe."

But Jungai was secretly worried because Matong had not returned.

That evening Jungai, Yindi and the other six cradle-flyers set off towards the farm, with Rufus swinging beneath in the cradle.

In a dark corner of the farmyard was Farmer Moody. He was convinced that the events of the previous night were not accidental. He crouched in the shadows, gun at the ready, eyes unblinking; watching and waiting. In a nearby tree another pair of eyes were watching the farmer; they were waiting too.

Yindi flew ahead of the cradle. Then she flew several times around the farm, staying in the cover of the trees. From this distance she could not see Moody hiding in the shadows and reported back to Jungai that the coast was clear.

Rufus sat in the cradle; nervous but also excited. They were going to rescue his friend.

Banjora waited expectantly in the top of his tree, unaware of Farmer Moody hidden below. He looked forward to jumping into the cradle and escaping. 'Easy as 1,2,3' or so he thought.

As the bats flew towards Banjora, Moody quietly raised his gun, smiling as his finger felt the trigger. '3, 2, 1 and bang,' he thought.

Then whack! His face was covered in something leathery. He could not see. The gun went off and he dropped it, clawing at whatever was wrapped around his head.

Big Rusty leapt from his kennel and started barking furiously, although he was not sure what he was barking at. Still, barking was fun. He barked even louder.

Jungai, hearing the shot, now saw Moody struggling with Matong; for it had been Matong, watching from the trees, who had acted to save the rescue team.

"Quickly, keep going… Banjora jump!"

On the ground Moody had wrenched Matong from his head and as the bat struggled to fly from the ground he picked up his gun and took aim. "Bye bye, bat."

Then whack, again. Yindi flew into his head, pulling his nightcap over his face. For the second time the gun went off. Yindi flew away to the cover of the trees as Moody dragged the cap from his eyes.

Matong had finally made it into the air but Moody had him in his sights. He aimed, smiling nastily. Click, click, click-click; but the gun failed to fire. It only had two shots and needed reloading.

Moody turned around and saw what looked like a giant multi-winged bat, silhouetted against the rising moon, flying away with something suspended beneath.

The enclosure was now empty.

"Curses!"

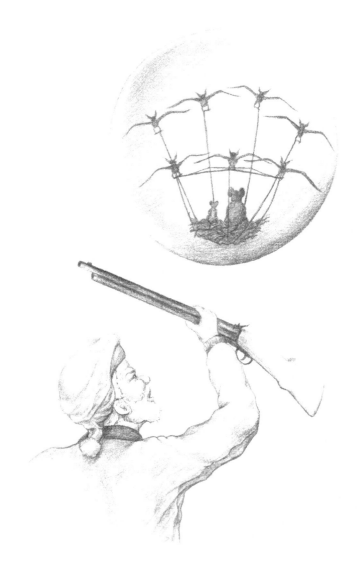

Moody threw his gun away in frustration. Unfortunately, it landed on Big Rusty. The poor dog had a headache for weeks.

Back at the old roost all the bats had returned safely with Rufus and Banjora. Matong's wings looked like a colander where the buckshot from Moody's gun had passed through them the night before. Very fortunately only the skin on his wings had been hit. He explained to the others why he had decided to hide nearby and keep watch. He knew that the Farmer was clever and might set a trap.

Matong said, "That was very brave of you, Yindi, to come to my rescue."

All the other bats together with Banjora and Rufus agreed and shouted "Hooray for Yindi!" which made her feel happy, despite her sadness at knowing she would soon say goodbye to her friend.

The next evening, fond farewells were made as the nine bats and Rufus and Banjora parted company. Matong and Yindi headed East towards the mountains and the Colony.

The others went West.

The seven young bats flew ever Westwards, with Banjora and Rufus swinging beneath them, snug in the flying-cradle. Soon they had left the forest behind and were flying over scrubland. In the distance, early morning sunlight glinted on a wide expanse of water. This was the Big-water Lake. It was deep and many kilometres across. Jungai called to the other six bats. "Are you OK to fly on, it looks very wide." They all felt tired but did not want to appear weak. "Fine, yes, yes," they replied. So, on they flew.

About three quarters of the way across a strong wind began to blow. It was almost directly against them and progress forward slowed noticeably. Rufus shivered and crawled into Banjora's fur. Now only female koalas have **pouches**[3], but Banjora had a fold of skin over his tummy and Rufus now pulled this over him like a pouch. Banjora did not mind. He had dim memories of once being warm and safe inside a pouch himself.

Jungai became worried for he was getting very tired and knew the others would be feeling the same. He looked back over the water reaching far behind them. He knew that even with the help of the wind they would find it hard to make it back to dry land.

"Keep going," he called out in desperation.

---

[3] **pouches** – new-born koalas stay in their mothers' pouch for about six months, until they are strong enough to survive outside. They spend another six months being carried on their mothers' back. At about one year old they can live independently.

"Look ahead. We are nearly there."

They struggled on. Banjora became very concerned, but Rufus slept on, untroubled by the drama that was unfolding. Suddenly one bat let go crying out an apologetic, "Sorry, too tired, have to go back."

Jungai yelled at the others, "Come on, keep strong, we can still make it!" more in hope than expectation.

Fortunately, Banjora spotted something familiar, a tall but dead looking tree. It was on a small island about four hundred metres away.

"Jungai, put us down in that tree over there, it's our only hope."

Jungai saw the tree and steered the others towards it.

It took a couple of attempts to deposit Banjora in the tree but once done the bats circled it a few times, not sure what to do. The wind gusted fiercely and Jungai made a decision.

"We must all fly back to find food and rest, but we will return for you soon, Banjora, so hold tight and don't worry."

Banjora climbed down to the only branch on the tree and watched the six bats, still holding the cradle, flying back across the lake until they disappeared from sight.

There was a stirring in his "pouch" and Rufus appeared. He rubbed his eyes and looked around.

"Hey mate, what are we doing here and where are the flyers?"

Banjora explained then added, "But don't worry they will be back."

Rufus crawled back into his "pouch" and both settled down to rest. The wind grew stronger as night fell.

In the morning, after Rufus had emerged, Banjora climbed down the tree to have a look at the island. He was disappointed to find that it was mud and quicksand which did not support his weight. He could not get to the water to drink. He struggled to get back to the tree. Getting a drink from the lake was out of the question. He explained the situation to Rufus, who despite this, went down to "Give it a go" but with the same result. He climbed back.

Banjora said, "We will be hot and dry…."

"Not to mention starving," interrupted Rufus.

"As I was saying, we will be hot and dry, but Jungai and the others will be back soon to take us on to the other side."

Banjora said these words confidently. He trusted Jungai.

Two nights passed, the wind continued to blow hard and Banjora was beginning to have doubts. Had Jungai and the others come to harm. This seemed to be the only explanation for their failure to return. Perhaps Rufus and he were now marooned on this island, up this ragged, lifeless, leafless tree.

Their plight had not gone unnoticed, however. On a nearby sandbank a group of Black-necked storks were resting after their morning feed.

"What do you call a female kangaroo paddling in the lake?" asked one.

"Dunno," said the rest.

"Henrietta, of course."

All the storks fell about laughing, kicking their long legs out and flapping their wings.

All, that is, except one. He was new to this area. He looked on at the crazy dance of the other birds, in bewilderment.

He was standing on a floating log just off the sandbank.

When the others had calmed down a bit, the new bird said, "I do not understand; why Henrietta?"

The log burst from the water, sending the bird tumbling as it roared out:

"Because Henry ate her. Ha-ha-ha!"

Henry was the king of all crocodiles who lived in the lake. He was more than three and a half metres long and no one, just no one, ever disagreed with him.

"I have a task for you," he said, fishing the bedraggled young stork from the water by a leg.

"See those creatures in that island tree?" the bird trembled and nodded. "I need to help them. I need someone to encourage them to come down so I can give them a lift to shore; because that's the sort of nice guy I am. Can you do that for me?"

"Yessir, yes lord, yes, yes but please let me go."

Henry dropped the stork from his huge mouth back into the water. It struggled to stand up. Once standing it retreated onto the sandbank.

"Well!" Henry roared, "get going before I change my mind and have you for a snack."

A few minutes later the stork flew to the top of the tree above Banjora. It's leg still hurt from being in the crocodiles' mouth but it managed to balance by flapping its' wings.

"Hey, you guys look a bit stuck. Don't know how you managed to get here, but more importantly do you know how you are going to get off?"

"Come to give us a ride mate," said Rufus, "most kind of ya."

"We are waiting for the friends that flew us here," said Banjora, "so we are fine thank you."

The bird flew down and landed on a familiar looking log and said,

"They are OK, just waiting for friends."

The log was in fact Henry, who had swum quietly over to the island. He resisted the urge to gulp this idiotic bird down, but instead said in his softest voice, albeit through clenched teeth (more than sixty-six of them.)

"Just convince them they need a lift and tell them I am waiting to help."

Banjora looked on, puzzled. The bird appeared to be talking to a log. When it flew back it explained that nothing was flying far because of the very strong wind, so their friends might be delayed for a long time. But kind Henry, the log like looking creature below, would be happy to help. He could get them to the shore in no time at all, where there was fresh water and food.

"We'll take it," said Rufus, setting off down the tree, ignoring Banjoras' calls to wait.

So it was that Rufus and Banjora found themselves seated on the head of Henry as he set off towards the shore.

"If you both sit a bit further forward I can see better," he almost simpered. "That's it, just a bit further forward, not long now."

'Not long now until I eat you,' is what Henry was actually thinking; whilst Banjora was beginning to relax. He was dry, comfortable and nearly ashore.

Then Henry flipped them both high into the air and with his gaping jaws pointed skywards, he waited for lunch to arrive. He had done this so many times before that he closed his eyes, knowing they would drop straight back in. Henry waited and waited. Then, opening his eyes, was astounded to see his lunch flying off towards the shore.

Roaring with disappointment and extreme rage, he went crazy, thrashing the lake into a frenzy of waves and spray.

All the lake creatures wisely retreated from his anger.

"Just in time I think," said Jungai.

He and the reunited flying team had arrived and caught Banjora and Rufus in the cradle, just before they fell back into Henry's cavernous mouth below.

They made it safely across the lake and flew on towards some distant woodland. The wind had dropped. Jungai explained that the wind had been blowing too strongly to fly into it and this had delayed their return.

"We couldn't believe it when we saw you riding on the nose of that croc. Whatever possessed you. Don't you know they are a very bad lot and how very devious and dangerous they are?"

"We do now," said Banjora and Rufus together.

The group stopped and rested in trees that evening. They found food and water and slept quite well. From time to time they were woken by the sound of noisy engines and bright lights.

"The monster-trail," muttered Rufus. "Waroo told me about this; we just have to follow it South to reach the human colony and the zoo."

"And more rescues?" questioned a sleepy Banjora.

"Nah, home I think mate. Home, ya going home."

This was the slightly muffled voice of Rufus who was squeezing back into Banjoras' "pouch."

The next evening, they followed the monster-trail, which you would recognise as a road, to the human colony. It was what the local humans called a very large town. In the middle of this town was a big park and, in the middle of this park was a small zoo.

They flew cautiously towards the zoo and circled above it. Some wallabies on the ground looked up, puzzled. What was that flying above? A kite, a plane….no!

"It's a flying koala."

The wallabies hopped around telling the rest of the animals in the zoo that a new species of flying koala was about to drop in.

Meanwhile, Jungai and the tired bats were pleased to see a large eucalyptus tree ahead. In it were some koalas. These had stopped feeding and looked on in disbelief as another koala dropped from a net being carried by fruit bats, into their tree.

Jungai had also spotted other bats in a netted enclosure and lead his flyers over to an adjacent tree.

"I need to speak to your Elders," he said to the bats inside.

"We can help you escape."

An Elder of the zoo colony approached.

"That won't be necessary my friend, we are safe here and well looked after. Why don't you join us?"

"No thanks, we must get back to our own Colony."

Jungai now realised how much he missed being with Yindi.

Over at the koala compound the excitement was great. A new member in the shape of a fine young, if a bit chubby, male had arrived. Rufus asleep in the "pouch" was the source of this chubbiness.

"Come meet the rest," said a kindly looking koala, who appeared to be their leader. His name was Palrurt. He led Banjora down the tree to where twelve other koalas were gathered.

"How long have you all been here?" asked Banjora.

"Some as long as sixteen summers, but my partner and I have been here for less than two. We were captured by poachers, but luckily they were caught by good humans who rescued us and brought us here. We are well cared for and therefore content."

He suddenly looked very sad. "Our regret is that our baby son was left behind and must have perished, for we were the last koalas in the area when we were captured."

Banjora could not believe what he was hearing. Was it possible that he had found his lost parents?

He stuttered, "If you met your son now, would you know him?"

"Most certainly," said Palrurt, "for he would have a star shaped birthmark, like this, on his right paw." He raised his paw.

Banjora raised his paw.

Amazingly, it had exactly the same mark.

"Dad, it's me, Banjora, your son, I've so much to tell you. But where is my Mum?"

"Here I am my son, I am right behind you." Her voice was so gentle, but it trembled with emotion. Then she started to sing softly. She was singing Banjoras' tune and that warm and safe feeling flooded over him as he hummed along with her.

The three hugged and talked and talked and hugged for hour after hour.

The following morning Jake and Zoe, the keepers at the zoo, were surprised to see seven fruit bats in a tree outside the bat compound. They quickly did a count and realised these had not escaped, but were from the wild. By late evening these visiting bats had gone, leaving behind a pile of twigs, branches and string.

"I doubt we will see those again," said Jake.

Zoe, didn't take in what Jake had said. She was puzzled and concerned. There was definitely one extra koala in the koala compound. It had not been there yesterday. It seemed to be a healthy young male, which was good news as they had a young female who needed a partner. A pair of older koalas seemed to have adopted this newcomer. She frowned. She would need to check it out and find how it had managed to get in.

She told Jake about the mysterious new arrival.

"Perhaps the bats flew him in," he joked.

Then, on seeing the concerned look on Zoe's face, quickly added,

"Don't worry, I'll go and check that their compound is secure, right now."

Jungai and the other wild bats came across in the evening to say their goodbyes. Banjora thanked them for their strength and bravery and wished them a safe journey back to the Colony.

"Give my love to Yindi and tell her I will never ever forget her, nor any of you. You saved me and now I am reunited with my parents."

These were his fond parting words as the bats took flight.

Banjora had been so caught up in the joy and emotion of finding his parents that he had completely forgotten about the sleeping Rufus.

When Rufus popped his head out, much to the surprise and laughter of the other koalas, Banjora felt suddenly, very deflated.

"I am so, so sorry Rufus, but the others have gone. How will you get home now?"

Rufus looked completely untroubled by this situation.

"No worries mate. I can stay with ya for a bit. I'll enjoy that. Then when I'm ready to go, there's a cousin of Waroo's here somewhere. He was too young to leave with him, but he should be ready by now. I'll look him up and we can go back overland together."

"It's time to feed my son."

Banjora's mother's voice called from above.

Banjora sighed; yes, all was well.

His dream of flying home had finally come true.

The author is a granddad and storyteller who lives in East Sussex. He has over the course of many years created spontaneous stories for the children in his life.

As they have now grown up it seemed apposite to put at least one of these stories into print, hopefully for other children to enjoy.

The illustrator is a talented young artist who lives to the South of London. Her ability to bring images to life with just pencil and paper was inspirational.

9 781786 236395